A Winter Tale

HOW RAVEN BROUGHT LIGHT TO THE WORLD

MARK E. TURNER

ILLUSTRATIONS BY
EMILY GRAVES

Stephen F. Austin State University Press
P.O. Box 13007, SFA Station
Nacogdoches, Texas 75962-3007
sfapress@sfasu.edu

LIBRARY OF CONGRESS-IN-PUBLICATION DATA
Turner, Mark
A Winter Tale / Mark Turner
Illustrations: Emily Graves

ISBN: 978-162288-032-4

1. Folktale. 2. Folktale - Alaskan. 3. Folklore- Native American

The paper used in this book meets the requirements of ANSI/NISO Z39.48-1992 (R 1997)(Permanence of Paper)

Production Location: Everbest Printing Co.
Guangdong, China Production Date 03/15/2014
Cohort Batch 1

Dr. Mark Turner holds a Bachelor of Music in Music Education from the University of North Texas, and a Masters and D.M.A in Music Education from the University of Houston.

Emily Graves graduated with a BFA in Commerical and Advertising Art in 2013 from Stephen F. Austin State University in Nacogdoches, Texas.

Many, many years ago, when Earth was created, there was no light. Darkness covered everything like a thick blanket.

People only knew the world as a cold and colorless place. This was the dark and lonely time. Happiness and joy could not take root without the warmth of light.

Families lived in harmony with nature, but they worked and played without the stars, the moon, the Aurora Borealis, or even the sun.

There was, however, one who didn't live in darkness. He was a greedy old chief who secretly kept the light of the world locked away from his people. He guarded this secret carefully, even from his own daughter.

But the Raven knew about the secret, and this is the tale of how the Raven tricked the old chief and brought light to the world.

Raven was a sneaky trickster, and he often peeked into people's homes to see what he could steal. One day, as Raven spied on the chief, he watched the old man creep to a corner of his house where he kept four decorated boxes. As the chief lifted each lid from each painted box, Raven saw shiny slivers of light struggling to escape their prisons.

For years, the selfish chief had hoarded the light, releasing its rays on rare occasions. Even then, he kept its power all to himself. Raven knew the old man would not willingly share the light, so he devised a plan to trick the chief into giving up his prized possessions.

The only thing more precious to the chief than his boxes of light was his daughter. Each day, the young woman took her basket to the river to fetch water for bathing and cooking.

One winter's day, Raven transformed himself into a very small spruce needle and floated into the water basket. When the young woman drank from the basket, she accidentally swallowed the spruce needle.

Once inside the young woman's stomach, Raven turned himself into a tiny baby boy and grew and grew and grew. The chief, in his old age, was delighted to have a grandchild to play with.

It wasn't long before the baby grew into a toddler and wanted to play with everything in his grandfather's house, including the ornately painted boxes.

For a while, the little boy was easily distracted from his grandfather's prized boxes, but as time passed, the boy's desire for the boxes increased. His whimpers became whines and his whines became wails—each more insistent and demanding than the last.

The boy's shrieks were as loud and piercing as the Raven's cry. Finally, his grandfather could take no more. Cautioning his grandson to take only a peek inside, the chief reluctantly offered him the box.

Once the little boy had the beautiful box in his hands, he joyfully tossed it into the air. Stars shot from the box, stippling the room and sky with light.

The world watched in wonder.

When the child saw the shimmering stars, he squealed and reached for another box. The old chief shook his head NO and frantically tried to amuse the boy with a buckskin ball. But the boy wanted nothing to do with the ball and hurled it at the remaining boxes.

This time, when the boy threw his tantrum, his cries were even more determined and deafening.

Again, the weary chief realized the only way to appease the boy was to let him look at another box. Slowly and carefully, the chief brought down a box, this one larger and more beautiful than the last. He sat next to the child with his treasure and again cautioned his grandson to take just a peek.

This time, the boy took one peek and then another; however, on the third peek, he tipped the lid off, and the carton flew from his hands.

he moon whooshed from the box to join the stars. The sky, once steeped in darkness, now glittered and glowed with light. People began to see the beauty of the world around them, and the little boy was both pleased and perplexed by their pleasure.

The old chief was distraught by the loss of his treasured moonlight and quickly collected all of the toys around the room in an attempt to distract his grandson from the two remaining boxes. The boy, however, wanted nothing to do with the toys and flung them at his grandfather's boxes.

Realizing his grandson could easily knock the remaining boxes off of the shelf, the chief took a third box down to satisfy the child. This time, the chief held the box himself and carefully cracked the lid so the boy could have a peek.

As soon as this unusual new light reached the child's eyes, he pushed the lid completely off of the box, letting the dazzling colors of the aurora glide across the sky.

People now praised their world in the glittering light of the stars, the calming glow of the moon, and the vibrant color of the Aurora. Again, the little boy was pleased. He realized light was good for the world. Now more than ever, he was determined to open the last box.

High on a shelf sat the largest and most ornately decorated box, and the boy imagined the light within it would be the biggest and best of all. Again, the young child screamed and shrieked and threw himself onto the floor, but the chief refused him the last box.

The boy did something desperate and held his breath until his face turned blue. Certain his blue-faced grandchild would die, the chief relented and brought down the last box from its safe and secure place.

The box sat on the floor and trembled. The chief and his grandson moved closer, and the box's movements turned frantic. Before the chief could secure the lid, the sun burst into the room and across the sky.

ow, the world was filled with light, and the satisfied child transformed himself back into a bird and flew away. The chief realized he had been tricked and chased after the Raven.

Ever since that day when the oceans began to hum and the mountains reached for the clouds, people have celebrated the Raven's gift and eagerly wait for all forms of light to brighten their hearts and homes.